BACKYARD MYSTERY

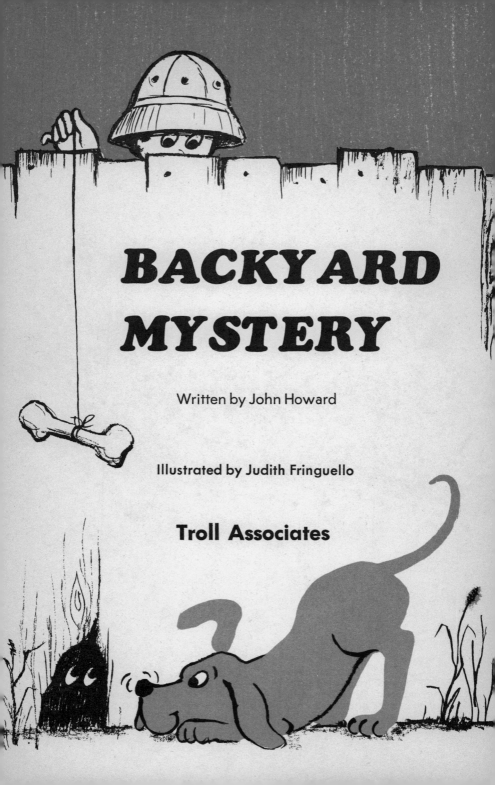

BACKYARD MYSTERY

Written by John Howard

Illustrated by Judith Fringuello

Troll Associates

The Backyard Mystery

When Jerry and Penny brought Gumdrop home for the first time, the stranger
was watching their every move.

"Roll over, Gumdrop. Roll over," Penny called.

Instead, the new puppy jumped up and raced around the yard. He was too busy exploring his new home to be bothered with tricks.

"Why is he watching us? That new boy keeps staring all the time," said Penny, looking up at the tree.

"Who knows," said Jerry, petting their new puppy. "Let's get the leash and take Gumdrop for a walk. Then he can't watch us."

They went inside the house for the new leash. They had spent the last of their allowances for a new leash and a collar.

"Mother, we're home," said Penny. "We have the new puppy. His name is Gumdrop."

"We're going to take him for a walk."

Gumdrop was playing in a corner of the backyard. He had an odd expression on his face, as if something had happened, and when Jerry reached down to clip the leash to Gumdrop's collar, he found that the collar was missing.

"Come on, Penny. Don't fool around.
Give me Gumdrop's collar."

"I don't have it, Jerry. Maybe it fell off.
It was kind of loose," said Penny.

They looked all over the yard. They hunted under bushes and behind trees. They even searched under flower pots, knowing all the time they were being watched.

Where could the missing collar be? They looked in the house, under the chairs and the sofa and the beds. Still they couldn't find it.

Finally Penny turned to her mother.
"Could he have chewed it up and swal-
lowed it?"

"Oh, I doubt that very much. Gumdrop's just a baby. Let me look. I'll find it," said Mother.

Mother spent a long time looking for the missing collar. She searched the house, the yard, and even in the garbage cans, but she couldn't find it either.

At last she said, "This is very strange. I guess we should take Gumdrop to the Vet to see if he really did chew it up and swallow it."

The Vet examined Gumdrop.

Then he took an X-ray of Gumdrop's stomach and developed the picture. "Obviously the missing collar is not here," said the Vet.

"Have you checked under bushes and trees, under flower pots and beds? These things do tend to turn up in yards and gardens, and even in garbage cans."

"I guess we'll have to stop at the store on the way home and buy a new collar," said Mother.

In the pet store, Mother handed over their next week's allowance while Jerry and Penny just looked at each other. How could they afford to keep buying new collars for Gumdrop?

"Okay," said Jerry when they got home. "This time I'll put Gumdrop's collar on him and we can start his training."

But Gumdrop didn't want to wear his new collar, and he didn't want to be trained. He wanted to play!

"Penny, try to get Gumdrop to come to you," said Jerry. "I'll get his leash. If we can get him to hold still, maybe we can start teaching him to obey."

Jerry disappeared into the house. In a minute he came running back.

"Where's the leash?" he called. "It's not on the hook. I bet you forgot to put it away yesterday."

"I did not forget," said Penny angrily. She walked over with Jerry to the back-door. "I remember putting it....LOOK. What's this? Look."

There, by the back door was the missing collar.

"How in the world did the missing collar get here?" asked Penny. "First it disappears and then it mysteriously appears. Now we've got two collars and no leash.

"Someone must be playing tricks on us. We have a real mystery to solve in our own backyard."

But Jerry wasn't listening to her. He was looking at the boy next door.

All through dinner Jerry thought and thought. Suppose someone **was** playing tricks. Could it be the new boy next door? He was always spying on them.

But why would he return the collar after he took it? And why would he take the leash? If only he could figure out what the new boy was planning to do next!

By bedtime Jerry finally had an idea that even Penny thought was good.

If the new boy thought they were leaving their house, he just might try to play another trick on them.

"Do you really think we can catch him?" Penny whispered excitedly. "If your idea works, maybe we can make him pay us back the money we had to spend for the other collar."

The next afternoon Jerry was ready to try his plan.

The new boy was watching Gumdrop playing in the backyard.

Now, they would spy on the new boy to see what he was really up to! This time they would catch him!

"GOODBYE, GOODBYE," they shouted as loud as they could. "GOODBYE, GOOD-BYE," they called, loud enough for the new boy to hear. "WE'RE GOING FAR, FAR AWAY."

They waved goodbye to Gumdrop and then walked slowly away.

As soon as they were out of sight, they scurried around to the back of their own backyard, careful not to be seen.

"Keep down, or he'll see you," whispered Jerry. "If he sees us, we'll never catch him."

Carefully, they peered through the bushes into their own backyard.

There was Gumdrop sniffing around the yard. And there was the new boy watching Gumdrop.

"Oh, Jerry, suppose he tries to take Gumdrop." Penny was frightened now.

"We'll catch him if he does," Jerry whispered back. "Shhh. Gumdrop's coming over
here." They held their breath.

Gumdrop stopped suddenly and began digging furiously in the ground. Scratch. Scratch. Scratch. Just then the new boy started to leap through the bushes toward Gumdrop.

"Do something, Jerry," cried Penny. But just as Jerry jumped up to grab the new boy, he saw what was in the hole Gumdrop was digging.

"Oh, no. You rascal! You're the one who's been hiding and burying things."

"Oh, Jerry. It was Gumdrop all the time. You really made a bad mistake," cried Penny.

"Me? It wasn't all my idea, you know. Anyway, it's Gumdrop's fault."

"Yes, Gumdrop, see what you made us do! You're a rascal."

Jerry turned to Penny. "You know, we've both been wrong. We've been thinking the wrong thoughts about the new boy just because we didn't get to know him. I think it's about time we said hello."

Just then the new boy walked over and shyly said, "Hello. My name is Charlie. I just moved in a couple of days ago. I've been watching your dog. He really likes to bury things in that hole, doesn't he? I think he buried my baseball."

Jerry and Penny could only look at each other and smile.

"Do you want to play in my tree house?" asked Charlie.

"WOW. What a tree house."

And while they played, what do you think
that rascal was doing?